T5-AQT-435

If You Hold My Hand

Written by Jillian Harker

Illustrated by Andy Everitt-Stewart

PaRRagon

Bath New York Singapore Hong Kong Cologne Delhi Melbourne

ROSE
COTTAGE

Jake's mom opened the front door. "Come on, Jake. Let's go outside and explore."

But Jake wasn't really sure. He was only small, and the world looked big and scary.

"*Only if you promise to hold my hand*," said Jake.

So Jake's mom led him down the long lane.
Jake wished he was back home again!

"This looks like a great place to play. Shall we take a look? What do you say?" asked Jake's mom.

"Only if you hold my hand," said Jake.

And Jake did it!

"Look at **me**! I can do it!" he cried.

"This slide looks like fun. Would you
like to try?" asked Jake's mom.

Jake looked at the ladder. It stretched
right up to the sky.

"I'm only small," said Jake. "I don't
know if I can climb that high—

unless you hold my hand."

And Jake did it!

"Wheee! Did you see me?" he cried.

"We'll take a shortcut through the woods," said Jake's mom.

"I'm not sure if we should," said Jake. "It looks dark in there. Well, I suppose we could—*will you hold my hand*?"

And Jake did it!

"Boo! I scared you!" he cried.

Deep in the woods,
Jake found a stream,
shaded by beautiful
tall trees.

"Stepping stones, look!"
said Jake's mom.
"Do you think you could jump
across these?"

"Maybe," said
Jake. "I just need you
to hold my hand, please."

And Jake did it!

One...

two...

three...

four....

"Your turn now, Mom," cried Jake,
holding out his hand.

Beyond the woods, Jake and his mom
ran up the hill, and all the way
down to the ocean.

"Come on, Jake," called his mom.

"Would you like to paddle in the sea with me?"

But the ocean looked **big**, and he was only small.

Suddenly, Jake
knew that didn't
matter at all.
He turned to
his mom and

smiled...

"I can do **anything** if you hold my hand," he said.